WELCOME TO
PASSPORT TO READING
A beginning reader's ticket to a brand-new world!

Every book in this program is designed to build read-along and read-alone skills, level by level, through engaging and enriching stories. As the reader turns each page, he or she will become more confident with new vocabulary, sight words, and comprehension.

These PASSPORT TO READING levels will help you choose the perfect book for every reader.

READING TOGETHER
Read short words in simple sentence structures together to begin a reader's journey.

READING OUT LOUD
Encourage developing readers to sound out words in more complex stories with simple vocabulary.

READING INDEPENDENTLY
Newly independent readers gain confidence reading more complex sentences with higher word counts.

READY TO READ MORE
Readers prepare for chapter books with fewer illustrations and longer paragraphs.

This book features sight words from the educator-supported Dolch Sight Words List. This encourages the reader to recognize commonly used vocabulary words, increasing reading speed and fluency.

For more information, please visit lbyr.com/passporttoreading.

Enjoy the journey!

Little, Brown and Company
Hachette Book Group
1290 Avenue of the Americas, New York, NY 10104
Visit us at LBYR.com

First Edition: April 2021

Little, Brown and Company is a division of Hachette Book Group, Inc.
The Little, Brown name and logo are trademarks of Hachette Book Group, Inc.

The publisher is not responsible for websites (or their content) that are not owned by the publisher.

Library of Congress Control Number 2021931266

ISBNs: 978-0-316-62793-1 (pbk.), 978-0-316-62790-0 (ebook), 978-0-316-62791-7 (ebook), 978-0-316-62792-4 (ebook)

PRINTED IN THE U.S.A.

CW

10 9 8 7 6 5 4 3 2 1

Passport to Reading titles are leveled by independent reviewers applying the standards developed by Irene Fountas and Gay Su Pinnell in *Matching Books to Readers: Using Leveled Books in Guided Reading*, Heinemann, 1999.

DREAMWORKS
Spirit
UNTAMED
FAST FRIENDS

Adapted by Rory Keane

LITTLE, BROWN AND COMPANY
New York • Boston

Attention, Spirit Untamed fans!
Look for these words
when you read this book.
Can you spot them all?

train

horse

saddle

frontier

This is Lucky Prescott.

She really loves the great outdoors,

and she loves going on

exciting adventures!

Lucky has a lot of animal friends,

but she wishes she had more

human friends.

Lucky lives in the big city
with her aunt Cora and her grandpa.
Aunt Cora wants Lucky to act like a lady.

Grandpa wishes Lucky could be
a little quieter.

One day, Lucky lets a squirrel into the house.
It is an accident,
but it ruins one of Grandpa's fancy parties.
Oh no!

Aunt Cora decides to take Lucky
on a trip out West.
They are going to live with Lucky's father
for the summer.

Lucky's father lives
in a small town called
Miradero.
His name is Jim.
He really loves trains.

Lucky's mother used
to live in Miradero, too.
Her name was Milagro.
She really loved to
ride horses.

Lucky takes a long train ride to Miradero.
She sees a galloping horse.

She calls him Spirit.
He is wild and free.

Lucky wants to be friends with Spirit when she gets to Miradero.

Her father says she cannot.
He does not think horses are
safe for her.

Lucky meets two girls in Miradero.

Their names are Pru and Abigail.

Abigail is really silly.

Her funny horse is called Boomerang.

Pru is a very good rider.

She even rides in the rodeo!

Her pretty horse is called Chica Linda.

Pru and Abigail know a lot about horses.
The girls know how to take care of them,
and they teach Lucky every step.

Abigail tells Lucky what to feed Spirit. Pru shows Lucky how to talk gently to Spirit.

At first, Spirit is very afraid of Lucky.
She takes her time with him.

She also gives him lots of apples to eat!
Yum!

Now Spirit trusts Lucky.

Lucky wants to ride Spirit.

It is not easy at first.

She falls off of his back a lot!

Ouch!

Pru and Abigail help Lucky try again.
Soon she knows how to ride a horse.

But Lucky rides a little differently
than Pru and Abigail.
She does not use a saddle like they do!

Pru, Abigail, and Lucky
ride their horses across the frontier.

They have fun and exciting adventures together!

The three girls are best friends before long. Together, Pru, Abigail, and Lucky are the PALs.

Chica Linda, Boomerang, and Spirit are pals, too!

Lucky loves living in Miradero with Spirit and her PALs!